## A Polish Up For Shelldon

Shelldon has lost his sparkle, so a trip to the Land of Spick 'n' Span is urgently needed!

The following names appearing in this publication:-

Shelldon™
Poke™
Footloose™
Tango™
Taps™
Tee-Ball™
Princess™
Belle™
Hummer™
The Hollow Tree™
The Kingdom of Keepsafe™

The Land of Lost™
Baron Von Clasp™
Don't Knowers™
Queen Cherish™
Princess Kee™
Nitelite™
Fancy™
Pearl™
Twist™
Hero™

Little League™
Perkins™
Keyboard™
Kazoo™
King Treasure™
King Collect™
Lose-It-Louie™
Metal Detectors™
The Don't Know Desert™
Prince Lockly™

are the trademarks of Tonka Europe Limited
under licence from Current Inc.

# A POLISH UP FOR SHELLDON

It was a dull, grey day in the Kingdom of Keepsafe. Shelldon, the turtle Keyper, was shuffling down the forest path, even more slowly than usual. His head hung down and he was plodding along very unhappily indeed.

At last he stopped beneath a big mountain ash tree and shook his head sadly.

"Hello, Shelldon," called Fancy the snail, coming out from behind the tree. She and her Finder, Footloose, had come to collect the tree's pale green leaves to make a picture. "What's the matter? You don't look very well. Even your shell looks dull today."

"I know," sighed Shelldon. "That's the trouble."

"I've lost the tin of special polish that I
keep to make my shell nice and shiny," he
sighed.

"It's not like you to lose something,
Shelldon," said Fancy.

"Why don't you look in your shell,
Fancy?" said Footloose, crawling out from
under the tree. "You might find something
in there that will do instead."

So Fancy opened her own jewel encrusted shell and began to rummage through all her fine bits and pieces inside. "Oh, this might be just the thing!" she cried, producing a little bottle of bright pink liquid. "Rose oil! I bought it from my friend the Rose Fairy."

"It was frightfully expensive – she's very top of the tree, you know – and it smells absolutely beautiful!" said Fancy.

"Shelldon doesn't want to smell beautiful!" snorted Footloose. "And besides look at it – it's pink! Whoever heard of a pink turtle shell?"

Fancy shut her shell with a click. "I was only trying to help," she sighed.

"Yes, of course," said Shelldon. "Oh dear. I feel so dull, and I'm supposed to be wise and sensible."

"Never mind," said Fancy. "Even sensible people lose things sometimes. We'll go and tell your Finder, Nitelite. He's a good Finder and so is Footloose – they'll soon find it for you."

"Just so long as Lose-it-Louie hasn't found it," muttered Footloose gloomily, as they set off down the forest path.

Nitelite was down at the Hollow Tree watching Tango, the ladybug, and Twist, her Finder, practising a dance.

"One, six, together, one, six, together," chanted Tango and Twist, trying not to tangle their eight legs.

They were all very surprised to hear Shelldon had lost something.

"And we're afraid Lose-it-Louie may have got it," sighed Shelldon.

"What was the polish made of?" asked Nitelite.

"The very best beeswax, of course, from my friends the bees, who live in the wild honey hives in the forest," said Shelldon.

HONEYCOMB

BEST HONE

BUMBLE'S
BEESWAX
POLISH

BEST HONEY

"You've no need to worry then," said
Nitelite. "Lose-it-Louie won't have taken
that!"

"Why not?" demanded Tango.

"He's too lazy," laughed Nitelite. "You
have to work hard to polish anything with
beeswax."

"Why didn't I think of that?" said
Shelldon.

"You're just not feeling too bright," said
Nitelite kindly. "You'll be all right after a
good polish."

"And I've a good idea where to find some of your special polish," Nitelite added.

"Where?" cried Fancy.

"In the Land of Spick 'n' Span, of course!" exclaimed Nitelite. "They just love polishing everything in sight there. They're never happier than when they're working hard making everything look nice. They're sure to have natural beeswax polish there."

BEE'S WAX

BEES MIX

"So come on everyone, into the Hollow
Tree. Let's go to the Land of
Spick 'n' Span and find some polish for
Shelldon," said Nitelite.

"One, six, together," chanted Tango and
Twist, as they danced into the Hollow Tree.

"Come on, Fancy, let's hit the trail!"
cried Footloose.

Fancy and Footloose entered the Hollow Tree, closely followed by Shelldon and Nitelite.

Inside the Hollow Tree, Fancy set the destination dial to the Land of Spick 'n' Span. Suddenly a whirl of colour swirled and twirled around the Finders and Keypers.

Before they knew it, the Hollow Tree and
everyone inside it had arrived in the Land
of Spick 'n' Span.

But as soon as they stepped out of the
Tree, they were nearly swept up! A busy
little street cleaner rushed at them with a
huge brush. "Keep the street tidy,
please!" he cried.

And he pointed to a piece of wool trailing from Fancy's shell. Before she could even try to put it away he had snipped it off with a pair of shiny shears, popped it in a paper bag, and rushed on.

Everybody got off the street and on to
some grass. But another busy person with
a brush rushed at them. "Please keep off
the grass," he cried. "You'll ruin it, walking
on it with all those feet," he added,
sweeping furiously where Tango had been
standing.

As the Keypers and their Finders walked on past all the clean and tidy houses, with their sparkling windows, they had to be very careful indeed. Those Spick 'n' Span folk were painting and polishing all over the place. And some of their tools seemed to work by themselves . . .

"I don't think I'd like to live here," said
Tango doubtfully.

"Oh, but it must look very nice when it's
all finished," said Fancy.

"I don't think they ever finish," said
Twist, glancing fearfully at a mop and
bucket that were marching along all by
themselves towards him.

Nitelite's keen eyes had spotted a shop that sold cleaning things. *The Clean Sweep*, said a sign. *Get your polish, sparkle, elbow grease, dusters and new brooms here.*

"In here, quick!" he cried. "We should be able to find some polish for Shelldon in this shop."

The shop bell jangled and a little old gnome came forward to serve them. Behind him were rows of tidily stacked shelves filled with cleaning things. And on the counter was a glass case labelled *Best Beeswax*. Inside were lots of shiny tins of beeswax polish, except for one that looked old and battered.

And then a very funny thing happened.
Before the gnome could speak, the old tin
suddenly grew arms and legs, climbed
down off its shelf, opened the case door
from the inside and leapt down on to the
counter.

"My tin of polish!" cried Shelldon.

The old gnome went very red.

"I didn't know it was your tin," he mumbled. "My cousin who lives in the forest of Keepsafe sends me a supply of beeswax polish from the wild honey hives there, and this time he added an old tin that he had found. Someone had left it lying around."

Shelldon looked at the gnome sternly. "He should have tried to find out whose it was," he said.

"I'm sorry. Please take it back," said the gnome. "And here's a present from me to help you rub it in." And he handed Shelldon a jar of green elbow grease.

Just then the Keypers heard the Hollow Tree calling that their time was up.

Quickly they rushed back to the tree,
who shut his door sharply on six brushes
that had chased them up the street.

The Hollow Tree was caught up in a
tumble of colour again and in a moment
they were back in the Kingdom of
Keepsafe.

As soon as they got out in Keepsafe, everybody set to work to polish Shelldon. And with the help of the elbow grease the gnome had given them, he was soon looking like his old sparkling self again.

"Now don't ever lose it, Shelldon," said Fancy. "We might get swept away altogether if we have to go to the Land of Spick 'n' Span again!"